ADDY McBEAN #1
Numbers Queen

BY
Margery Cuyler

ILLUSTRATED BY
Stacy Curtis

ALADDIN QUIX
New York London Toronto Sydney New Delhi

To Tim, numbers whiz

—M. C.

For the students, teachers, and staff
at Alice Gustafson Elementary School
Go, Gators!

—S. C.

This book is a work of fiction. Any references to historical events, real people, or real places are used fictitiously. Other names, characters, places, and events are products of the author's imagination, and any resemblance to actual events or places or persons, living or dead, is entirely coincidental.

ALADDIN QUIX
Simon & Schuster Children's Publishing Division
1230 Avenue of the Americas, New York, New York 10020
First Aladdin QUIX hardcover edition July 2024
Text copyright © 2024 by Margery Cuyler
Illustrations copyright © 2024 by Stacy Curtis
Also available in an Aladdin QUIX paperback edition.
All rights reserved, including the right of reproduction in whole or in part in any form.
ALADDIN and the related marks and colophon are trademarks of Simon & Schuster, LLC.
Simon & Schuster: Celebrating 100 Years of Publishing in 2024
For information about special discounts for bulk purchases, please contact
Simon & Schuster Special Sales at 1-866-506-1949 or business@simonandschuster.com.
The Simon & Schuster Speakers Bureau can bring authors to your live event. For more
information or to book an event contact the Simon & Schuster Speakers Bureau
at 1-866-248-3049 or visit our website at www.simonspeakers.com.
Designed by Laura Lyn DiSiena
The illustrations for this book were rendered digitally.
The text of this book was set in Archer Medium.
Manufactured in the United States of America 0624 LAK
2 4 6 8 10 9 7 5 3 1
Library of Congress Control Number 2023050956
ISBN 9781534489578 (hc)
ISBN 9781534489561 (pbk)
ISBN 9781534489585 (ebook)

Cast of Characters

Addy McBean: Second grader at PS 8 who loves numbers

Mom: Addy's mother; librarian at South Summit Public Library

Minus: Addy's dog

Dad: Addy's dad; coding genius who lives in San Francisco

Star Atlas: Addy's best friend

Ms. Atlas: Star's mother; works at PS 8

Mr. Vertex: Addy's teacher at PS 8

Latoya: Addy's classmate

Akim: Addy's classmate

Willard Gluck: Addy's classmate and Math on the Move partner

Maya: Addy's classmate

Bob: Addy's classmate

Ms. McGrath: Mr. Vertex's teaching aide

Carlos: Addy's classmate

Collin: Addy's classmate

Maria: Addy's classmate

Satchel: Addy's classmate

Max: Addy's classmate

Mita: Addy's classmate

Ms. Ralston: Principal at PS 8

Contents

Chapter 1: Countabunga! 1

Chapter 2: Addy's New Partner 10

Chapter 3: Addy's List 18

Chapter 4: Willard's Idea 27

Chapter 5: Reach for the Stars 40

Chapter 6: Disaster Strikes 49

Chapter 7: The Eleventh Hour 58

Chapter 8: Setting Up 70

Chapter 9: Math on the Move 77

Word List 85

Questions 88

1

Countabunga!

Addy McBean lives with **Mom** and their poodle, **Minus**, at 100 Division Drive, South Summit, New Jersey. Addy is nuts about her address because she's nuts about numbers.

She loves math just like **Dad**, who is a **coding** genius. He lives and works in San Francisco—2,887 miles away. Addy's parents are divorced, but she texts her dad all the time on her smart watch.

Addy to Dad:

I am minus one workbook, one Rubik's Cube, and one toothbrush.

Dad to Addy:

I bet you ten dollars that Minus took them.

Look under your bed.

Sure enough, when Addy pushes

aside three pairs of socks and one box of dominoes, she finds them.

Countabunga! That is Addy's favorite **expression**.

She says it when she's excited.

Addy likes to count things in their condo. She counts her footsteps when she walks Minus and the cornflakes in the cereal box. She also counts the books on the floor around her mom's bed.

Addy's mother is a librarian at the South Summit Public Library. She brings home great books for Addy to read.

After school on Monday the doorbell rings while Addy is feeding Minus.

She looks out the window and sees

Star Atlas. Star lives only two blocks away, and they've been best friends forever. Addy thinks it's funny that Star's last name is Atlas since Star likes maps. She even has a globe in her bedroom that lights up.

Star's eyes are flashing alarm when Addy opens the door.

She rushes into the hallway.

"What's wrong?" asks Addy.

"You can't believe what Mom just told me!" exclaims Star.

Ms. Atlas works

in the principal's office at PS 8. She finds things out before they happen.

"It's about **Mr. Vertex**," Star blurts out. "Tomorrow he's assigning an important math project. He wants us to work with new partners. That means we'll have to split up!"

Addy's heart skips three beats.

"But we are a one-plus-one team," she says.

"I know," says Star. "Remember the pumpkin **catapult** we made for our Halloween project?"

"And that picture we drew of how

we'll look at one hundred years old? It was a big hit on Hundredth Day," says Addy. "Maybe Mr. Vertex will change his mind."

"I doubt it," answers Star. "My mom says Mr. Vertex wants his students to work with different people." Star walks toward the front door. "I can't stay. Dad's waiting to help me with my homework."

During dinner Addy tells Mom about Mr. Vertex's plan.

"That's too bad," says Mom. "But

maybe you'll get a new partner who likes math as much as you do."

Addy is still a wreck. What if she ends up with someone who hates math? Or with one of the boys who call her Beanpole?

When she goes to bed, she counts by tens to one hundred, since that usually helps her fall asleep.

But not tonight. Addy can't stop thinking about what will happen at school the next day.

2

Addy's New Partner

When the two friends get to school, Mr. Vertex greets them at their classroom door. He's wearing his tie with numbers on it. His sneakers are covered with 3D shapes that flash on and off.

"Good morning, girls!" he says. "What do you call a hen who counts her eggs?"

For five seconds Addy forgets that she's mad at Mr. Vertex. She actually loves his math riddles. "An egg-static chicken?" she asks.

"Good guess," says Mr. Vertex, laughing. "But the answer is a 'mathema-chicken.'"

Addy and Star roll their eyes and trot to the math center. **Latoya** is measuring the lines of two squares to make sure they're equal. **Akim** is drawing a large blue trapezoid.

After the second bell everyone stands for the Pledge of Allegiance. Then Mr. Vertex makes the V sign. "I have an important announcement," he exclaims.

Here it comes, thinks Addy. *The important announcement that will ruin my life.*

"Next Tuesday evening is Family Night," Mr. Vertex continues. "That's one week from today. This year's theme is Math on the Move. All grades will display math projects in the gym for families to enjoy. Since we've been studying 2D and 3D shapes, we'll focus on those."

Mr. Vertex pauses, then continues, "I'll assign each of you a partner after we review shapes today. During math tomorrow you can brainstorm with your partner. Then the fun will begin! Your project must be finished by Monday afternoon for

setup. Have any questions?"

Addy raises her hand.

"Yes, Addy?" says Mr. Vertex.

"May Star and I be partners?" she asks.

"Not this time, Addy," he answers. "I've decided to mix and match. It's a good way to get to know a classmate you haven't worked with before."

Addy groans. She glances at Star, whose mouth looks like an upside-down semicircle.

As Mr. Vertex reviews 2D and

3D shapes on the whiteboard, Addy can barely concentrate.

"Can anyone give me an example of a **sphere** from real life?" asks Mr. Vertex.

Addy almost falls off her chair when **Willard Gluck** raises his hand. He doesn't like math. He doesn't even fill out his math worksheets. His math journal is a mess.

"Our eyeballs are spheres," he says.

What kind of weird answer is that? wonders Addy.

"That's a very creative—and correct—answer," says Mr. Vertex.

Finally it's time for their teacher to announce each person's partner.

Star is assigned to Latoya, another math lover. **Maya** and **Bob** are paired.

Then Mr. Vertex points to Addy and Willard. "I want you to work together," he says.

What?! Am I really stuck with Willard? Addy wants to sink into the floor and disappear forever.

3

Addy's List

During recess Star follows Addy to the swings. "I bet you'll be the one who comes up with your project idea," she says. "Willard's not exactly a math whiz."

"I know! I can't believe it. Maybe

while we're on the swings, you can help me think of a way out of this mess," Addy says. "I don't know what to do."

"Sorry, Addy. I promised Latoya I'd jump rope with her. See you later, alligator." Off she zooms.

Maybe I'll lose my best friend too, thinks Addy. *This day is awful.*

< >

When Addy gets back to class, Mr. Vertex and **Ms. McGrath**, the class aide, have moved Addy's desk to be opposite Willard's.

Addy thinks that with his springy hair, Willard looks a little like Minus.

Addy takes a deep breath. "Let's each think of some ideas before we brainstorm tomorrow," she says.

Willard answers quickly, "I don't have any ideas."

"Well, maybe you'll come up with some tonight," says Addy.

"I'll try," says Willard, "but crafts

aren't my thing. You'll have to do most of the work."

< >

The second Addy gets home, she drops her backpack onto a kitchen chair. Before yelling to her mom that she's home, she texts her dad.

Addy to Dad:

SOS. SOS. SOS.

Mr. Vertex won't let Star and me be partners on a math project for Family Night.

He says I HAVE to work with Willard Gluck.

We're studying shapes, and Willard says eyeballs are spheres.

I think that's weird.

Dad to Addy:

Change can be good.

New people have new ideas.

Eyeballs are spheres, right?

Addy to Dad:

I don't like change. I like things to stay the same.

No surprises.

Dad to Addy:

That's like your mom.

Don't forget, numbers can change.

Adding one number to another number makes a new number.

Addy stops texting. *Even Dad doesn't understand how I feel.*

"How did things go at school?" Addy's mom asks as she comes into the kitchen. "Who did Mr. Vertex assign as your partner?"

"Willard Gluck!" exclaims Addy. "He has *no* imagination, and he doesn't like math *or* crafts."

"Maybe your teacher hopes your math skills will rub off on him," Mom says, pouring two glasses of lemonade.

As she slowly sips her drink,

Addy scratches Minus's ears and thinks about the Math on the Move theme. Before she knows it, ideas pop in her brain like popcorn.

Addy runs to her desk. She grabs a pencil and a piece of paper. She writes down five vehicles that are "on the move." All five would be easy to make out of shapes.

Addy can't wait to get to school tomorrow. Even if Willard shows up with zero ideas, she's sure he'll go for the ones on her list.

4

Willard's Idea

When Addy and Star get to school the next day, Mr. Vertex is his usual smiley self.

"I have a new riddle: What number can you multiply by any number to get the same answer?" he asks them.

"**ZERO!**" both friends shout.

"Correct," says Mr. Vertex, giving them each a sticker for knowing the right answer.

Star goes to meet Latoya at the math center, and they begin moving eight 2D shapes around on the table. Addy looks at her two classmates, wishing she could join their team. She goes over to her desk, checks her watch, and waits **impatiently** for Willard.

Mr. Vertex walks over before the second bell rings. "Willard's absent

today, Addy," he tells her. "He has a peanut allergy, and he ate something that set it off. He won't be back in school till tomorrow."

Allergic to peanuts just like he's allergic to math, thinks Addy.

"I've written down five ideas

to share with Willard," she says. "If we can't brainstorm till tomorrow, how are we going to settle on a project and finish it by Monday?"

"May I see your list?" asks Mr. Vertex. Addy anxiously hands it to him.

"These are great," says Mr. Vertex. "I hope Willard will contribute some too. Just keep it simple, like your cart idea."

What if Willard doesn't like my cart idea? worries Addy. And *what if I don't like his ideas? Not that he'll have any.*

Addy feels like a lump of cold oatmeal all morning. She feels even worse when Star tells her at lunch about how excited she is to work with Latoya. "We're making a map of our town's main street."

"Was that your idea?" asks Addy.

Star smiles and nods.

< >

After school, as Ms. Atlas is driving the girls home, they pass Willard's house.

BRAIN FLASH! BRAIN FLASH! BRAIN FLASH!

Addy leans over the front seat and yells into Ms. Atlas's ear. "Can you pull over for a minute?"

"Are you going to throw up?" asks Star's mom, **swerving** to the curb.

"No, I just want to visit Willard. We couldn't brainstorm today, but now I hope we can." Addy uses Ms. Atlas's phone to call and tell her mom that she's stopping at Willard's. Mom says she'll pick Addy up later.

Addy jumps out of the car and

races to Willard's front door. She presses the doorbell one, two, three times.

Willard swings open the door. His face is covered with blotchy, red spots.

Addy starts to count them but stops when Willard exclaims, "What are you doing here?"

"I came to see if you've come up with ideas for our project. If we figure out what to make now, we can work on it tomorrow. What did you eat that gave you those spots?"

"I ate store-bought hummus. It had

a trace of peanuts in it, so I broke out in a rash. I had to get a shot, and I couldn't go home until my rash began to fade. I feel pretty good now, so you can come inside. My parents are upstairs."

Addy glances around the hall and notices photographs of rockets and space shuttles. A mobile of sixteen stars hangs from the ceiling. She peeks into the family room. There's a huge sculpture of a bumpy-looking rock.

"That's an asteroid. My parents are **astrophysicists**," Willard explains.

"What's an astro . . . whatever?" asks Addy.

"Astrophysics is a science that uses physics and chemistry to study objects like asteroids in our solar system," says Willard.

Addy's eyebrows shoot up in surprise. She's never heard Willard use such big words.

"And guess what? I have an idea for our project," says Willard.

"And I have five ideas," says Addy. She pulls her list out of her backpack and hands it to Willard.

After eyeballing it, Willard says, "Good try, but I bet other kids have thought of the same things."

Addy's stomach feels a little jumpy. She was sure Willard would like her suggestions.

"My ideas are about things that move. They match the Math on the Move theme," says Addy.

"Well, I think my idea is better," says Willard.

He walks to the printer in the family room, lifts out a piece of paper, and hands it to Addy. The paper has a colorful photograph of the solar system on it. She counts one sun and eight planets. Plus she sees thousands of stars.

"The photo doesn't show the almost three hundred moons that have so far been discovered in our solar system," says Willard. "Unfortunately, we won't have time to add them."

"You mean our project should be a drawing of the solar system?"

"More like a model of spheres, since planets and the sun are round," says Willard. "To pick up on your idea, they are also on the move. They spin on their axes."

Addy starts to imagine what a model of the solar system might look like. She can see the whole thing in her head. Planets made from colored clay. The sun a big yellow sphere. This project could be really fun.

"Countabunga!" Addy exclaims with a smile. "Let's go for it!"

5

Reach for the Stars

Addy's mom picks Addy up at Willard's and hands her a library book. It's called *Ada Byron Lovelace and the Thinking Machine.*

"Ada Lovelace wrote the first computer program almost two

hundred years ago," says Mom.

"Maybe someday I'll be a famous mathematician too," muses Addy.

"Anything's possible, if you reach for the stars," says Mom.

"What does that mean?" asks Addy.

"It means you should work hard to meet a challenge, no matter how difficult."

"That's what Willard and I will do!" exclaims Addy.

She tells her mom about her visit with Willard and how his parents are astro-fizzies. Then she texts to update her dad.

Dad to Addy:

You sound over the moon.

Addy to Dad:

We'll reach for the stars.

< >

When Addy gets to class the next morning, she looks around for Willard. Just as everyone stands for the Pledge, he dashes into the room and stands stiffly by his desk.

"I'm glad you've recovered, Willard," Mr. Vertex says. "Addy brought in a list of ideas. Do you have any you want to add?"

"Actually, Addy dropped by my house yesterday, and we've agreed on a spheres project," says Willard. "We want to make a model of the solar system."

"Great concept!" exclaims Mr. Vertex.

Addy and Willard rush to the art table. **Carlos** and **Collin** are painting seven boxes that are different shapes and sizes. One is red, two are yellow, two are purple, and two are lime green.

"We're making a giant alien out of boxes," explains Carlos.

Maria and **Satchel** are painting what looks like a barn. It has rectangular sides, square ends, and a triangular roof. "We're making a **diorama** of a farm," says Satchel.

Max and **Mita** are painting little rectangles a bright yellow.

"We're making the Yellow Brick Road from *The Wizard of Oz*," explains Mita.

Mr. Vertex gives Addy and Willard a large piece of cardboard, one paintbrush, one can of black paint, and two aprons.

"I'll paint half, and you paint half," suggests Willard.

"I'd rather roll clay into the shapes of the planets," says Addy.

Ms. McGrath has been listening. "You should make the planets tomorrow after the cardboard has dried. That way the clay will still be soft enough to attach to the cardboard."

Addy really likes Ms. McGrath. She always has helpful ideas when it comes to crafts.

"Okay, here goes," says Willard. He waves his brush in the air and then shoves it into the black paint.

SPLAT!

Half the paint lands on the table.

"I told you crafts aren't my thing," says Willard, waving his brush around some more. A big blob of paint lands in Addy's hair. Another blob splashes the box that Carlos and Collin are painting.

"Hey, watch it," yells Collin.

Willard's glasses and T-shirt are now splattered with gloppy paint. Addy grabs the paintbrush. "I think I'd better do the painting."

"You can't say I didn't warn you,"

Willard cries, yanking off his glasses.

Ms. McGrath takes Willard to the sink and helps him clean up.

Addy looks at the mess on the table. *Willard might have a good brain, but crafts are DEFINITELY not his thing. I'll have to reach for the stars all by myself!*

6

Disaster Strikes

When Willard arrives at school the next day, he smiles at Addy and holds up a paper bag.

"I made some little rings out of wire last night to add to Saturn, Uranus, Jupiter, and Neptune," he explains. He turns the bag over, and the rings spill onto his desk.

"I'm sorry about yesterday," he continues. "I'm going to try harder. I brought in the photograph of the solar system, so we'll know where to place everything."

Willard is trying, thinks Addy. *He thought about the rings. Maybe I should give him another chance.*

They spend math time working with their heads close together. Addy rolls different colors of clay into the round shapes of the planets.

She makes a beautiful yellow ball for the sun.

Willard places everything exactly where it should go. He adds the wire rings to the four planets. Ms. McGrath helps them attach the clay spheres to the cardboard that is the base for the solar system.

"Now your spheres won't roll away," she says.

"On Monday we can tape down labels," says Addy. "I'll print them out this weekend."

"Great, since I won't be around,"

says Willard. "I'll be in Brooklyn celebrating my bubbe's sixtieth birthday."

Addy can't wait till the weekend. Then she'll have more time to study the planets.

Finally, on Sunday afternoon, Mom lends Addy her laptop. Addy's heart races when she discovers how far each planet is from the sun. So many beautiful, long numbers! She prints them out. Maybe she'll have room to add the miles below the labels.

She texts the list to her dad.

Dad texts back:

You're zeroing in on the finish line!

Addy to Dad:

I wish you'd come for Family Night.

OOOXXX LOL

Addy feels a little stab in her

heart when she writes that. It hurts that her dad lives so far away.

< >

On Monday, Willard doesn't show up at school. *Of all days to be absent,* thinks Addy. *I bet he ate a peanut!*

Just then Willard rushes into the classroom. "I'm sorry that I'm late," he tells Mr. Vertex. "I overslept."

Willard dumps his backpack onto his desk and races to the art table.

CRASH!

He trips over the boxes on the floor and knocks the table sideways.

The can of orange paint tips over, spreading a river of orange across the solar system.

"Oh no!" screeches Addy. She bursts into tears.

Mr. Vertex and Ms. McGrath rush over. Collin and Carlos freeze, their mouths hanging open. The other kids grab paper towels and start blotting the paint, which just makes things worse. Willard **frantically** tries to wipe paint from his shirt, arms, and glasses. *He looks like an alien too,* thinks Addy.

Willard goes to the nurse's office for a change of clothes. Mr. Vertex tells Addy to take a book and walk to the quiet corner. "You can stay there till you feel better."

Star throws her a sympathetic look, but Addy ignores it. She can't believe the solar system is ruined. Now they'll have no project for Family Night.

It's all Addy can do to get through the rest of the day. She doesn't want to talk to anyone, not even to Star, and especially not to Willard.

What a disaster!

7

The Eleventh Hour

When Addy gets home, she goes to her room with Minus. They both plop down onto Addy's bed. In less than three minutes Addy falls asleep.

An hour later Mom knocks on

her door. She sits down on Addy's bed and gives her a long hug. "Mr. Vertex called me and told me what happened. I'm so sorry. I know how excited you were about your solar system."

Addy starts crying again, but then the doorbell rings. Her mom leaves to see who's there.

It's Willard!

"I HAVE to talk to Addy **RIGHT NOW**, Ms. McBean," he says. **"It's URGENT."**

"She just woke up," says Mom. "I don't think she's ready for a visitor."

"This can't wait," says Willard.

"It's okay, Mom. I'm ready," Addy announces as she slowly **descends** the stairs. Willard is standing in the hall with a box, shifting back and forth from one foot to the other.

"You probably don't want to see me right now," he says, "but I have a great idea that will fix everything."

Addy is speechless as he lifts out what looks like a metal helmet. There's a dial on top and a nozzle that sticks out beneath it. Willard pulls a red balloon from his pocket.

"For my bubbe's birthday my mom and dad used this **helium** tank to blow up sixteen balloons. They looked amazing—sixteen perfect ovoids."

Willard wants us to do an ovoid

project? Ovoids—3D oval shapes—are kind of like spheres, but we've run out of time.

"No, no, no," cries Addy. "It's too late."

"But this is a quick and easy fix," says Willard. "My parents taught me how to use the tank. It will take us about ten minutes to blow up all these balloons."

Addy's mind turns in circles. Things that are good have become bad and then good and then bad again. She got stuck with Willard as her partner (bad). Willard had a great idea (good). Willard was a messy painter (bad). Addy made perfect planets and a sun (good). Willard ruined their project (bad). Now Willard has a new idea (good?).

"If it's as easy as you say, I guess it's worth a try," says Addy. "But won't we still have to tie the end of each balloon after it's blown up? And won't we need string to tie to the ends as well? Otherwise, how will we carry the balloons into school?"

"Do you have any string?" asks Willard.

Addy fetches string and scissors, while Willard empties his pockets and spreads sixteen balloons on the floor by the tank. While it takes ten minutes to inflate the balloons, it takes almost fifteen minutes to knot the ends and tie on the strings. Finally, though, all sixteen balloons are blown up and bouncing around on the ceiling.

Addy looks up, and her shoulders sag. "I wish we could do something to make the balloons

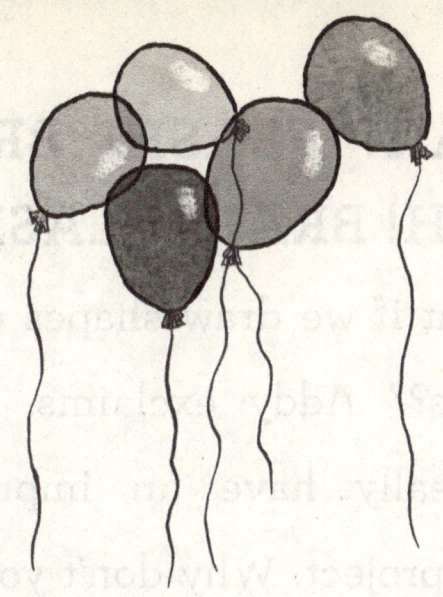

more interesting," she says. Then her eyes rest on the box of markers by the phone on the hall table.

BRAIN FLASH! BRAIN FLASH! BRAIN FLASH!

"What if we draw shapes on the balloons?" Addy exclaims. "Then we'll really have an impressive shapes project. Why don't you stay for dinner, and we'll finish up?"

Did I really just invite Willard Gluck to dinner? Addy wonders.

Willard smiles. "Awesome! I'm sure my parents will say yes."

< >

After dinner they begin to draw. Addy looks over and sees Willard

making a circle on top of a square. Then hair made of **spirals** on top of the circle. Then spindly legs at the bottom of the square made of thin rectangles. For shoes he draws circles. He adds a face made of more circles, a triangle, and a curved line.

"*What* are you doing?" asks Addy.

"Jazzing things up a bit. After all, our theme is Math on the Move. My square needs to look like it can run."

Willard's drawing is much cooler than my hexagram, Addy admits to herself. She grabs a marker and adds a triangular skirt to her hexagram. Then one circle on top of another for legs, and an octagon for a face.

Addy and Willard experiment with different colors and the shapes that they've learned. When they've covered all the balloons with drawings, they stand back to look at their work.

"Not bad for a project at the eleventh hour," says Addy.

"We're in good shape!" exclaims Willard. "I'll meet you outside school tomorrow to help carry the balloons inside. I promise I won't be late."

For the first time in a week, Addy has a good night's sleep.

8

Setting Up

Tuesday morning Addy wakes up thirty minutes early to get herself—and the balloons—ready. First she unties the strings from where she wrapped them around a chair. Then she holds them tightly in her fist as she walks to the front door. The balloons bump against the sides of the door as she pulls them through. **POP** goes a purple balloon.

"Oh no," cries Addy. "Now we're minus one balloon."

She stands at the end of the driveway as Star and her mom pull up.

"What are you doing with all those balloons?" Ms. Atlas asks as she and Star leap out of the car.

"They're Willard's and my math

project for Family Night," explains Addy.

"Wow!" exclaims Star. "You worked fast. Let me help you with those."

The girls struggle to push the balloons into the back of the car. Then they crawl in below. The balloons bob against the backs of the girls' heads, but Ms. Atlas makes it to the entrance of PS 8 in plenty of time. Star pushes and Addy pulls. Somehow they get the balloons out of the car while managing to hold on to the strings.

Willard is sitting on a bench by the front entrance. Addy can't believe he actually made it to school early.

Addy hands Willard her bunch. "A purple balloon popped, but otherwise they're all here," she says.

"Thanks," says Willard. "We should head straight for the gym and figure out where to put them. All the other Family Night projects must already be set up."

"How're we going to **anchor** the balloons in place, so they won't float away?" asks Addy.

Willard smiles. "I already thought of that. I brought rocks in my backpack. We can set them on top of the strings."

Two Willard surprises in one day, thinks Addy.

The balloons sway back and forth as they walk to the gym. Tables are arranged in long rows. When they find the second-grade aisle, Willard and Addy quickly set up their project.

Addy looks around. Carlos and Collin's giant alien looks great, considering they had to repaint the boxes after Willard's accident.

Star and Latoya's map of South Summit's main street is fabulous. Addy thinks their balloon project is kind of simple compared to everyone else's. *I wish we had finished the solar system, but at least we completed the assignment. I feel good about that,* thinks Addy.

9
Math on the Move

When Addy gets home that afternoon, a huge bunch of balloons addressed to her is in the kitchen. *Who sent these?* wonders Addy. Then she reads the card.

One hundred kisses from Dad.

A bunch of balloon love! thinks Addy. *Now I feel better. Maybe our balloons aren't so boring after all.*

< >

When Addy and her mom walk into the gym that evening, Addy is amazed by how awesome the displays look. Everything appears different at night, and even kind of magical.

Addy and Mom walk around, admiring all the projects. As they stop in front of some fifth-grade Popsicle-stick airplanes,

Addy hears laughter. Then a **"Watch out!"** and "Balloons are out to get you."

She looks up and sees—not just any balloons but hers and Willard's floating toward the ceiling. She dashes back to the second-grade aisle and finds Willard standing there . . . laughing!

"What's so funny?" asks Addy. "We have another disaster on our hands!"

Willard can hardly speak since

he's laughing so hard. "It's not a disaster at all! Our balloons actually *are* Math on the Move! I guess the rocks didn't work, but that's a good thing."

It takes a minute for Willard's words to sink in. But then Addy starts laughing as hard as Willard is.

Later that night Star and Latoya are awarded first prize for the best second-grade project. Collin and Carlos get second prize for their giant alien. Two kids in the other

second-grade class get third prize for a freight train.

Next **Ms. Ralston**, the principal, makes a surprise announcement. "We're awarding a merit prize to second graders Addy McBean and Willard Gluck. Their solar-system project was ruined yesterday due to an accident. Even so, they got together last night and came up with the wonderful balloon project on our ceiling."

Addy is stunned. She looks at Willard, whose face is the color of a red balloon.

I guess that's three Willard surprises in one day, she thinks, smiling broadly at him.

< >

That night Addy gets into bed and hugs her pillow.

She counts the good things that have happened to her in the past week.

1. Dad sent her a bunch of balloon love.

2. The balloon project got a merit prize.

3. Willard is not the kind of person Addy thought he was.

4. Star is still her BF, despite having been Latoya's partner.

5. Best of all, Addy has learned that things don't always turn out the way you expect, and that's okay.

Countabunga!

Word List

anchor (ANG•kur): To keep something in place with a heavy object

astrophysicists (a•struh•FIH•zuh•sist): Scientists who study objects in outer space

catapult (KA•tuh•pult): A machine for launching objects

coding (KOH•ding): Writing for computer systems

descends (dih•SENDS): Moves down

diorama (die•uh•RAH•muh): An exhibit with people, animals, or objects representing a scene

expression (ex•PREH•shun): An important word or phrase

frantically (FRAN•tih•klee): In a fast and nervous manner

helium (HEE•lee•um): A gas used to filled balloons

impatiently (ihm•PAY•shunt•lee): In a restless manner

sphere (SFEER): A round object where every point on the surface is the same distance from the center

spirals (SPY•ruhls): Curved, curly shapes

swerving (SWUR•ving): Suddenly turning aside from a straight course

Questions

1. Why does Addy like having Star as her partner?
2. What does "reach for the stars" mean?
3. What kinds of scientists are Willard's parents?
4. Is Addy a good partner to Willard?
5. What disasters happen to Addy and Willard's projects?